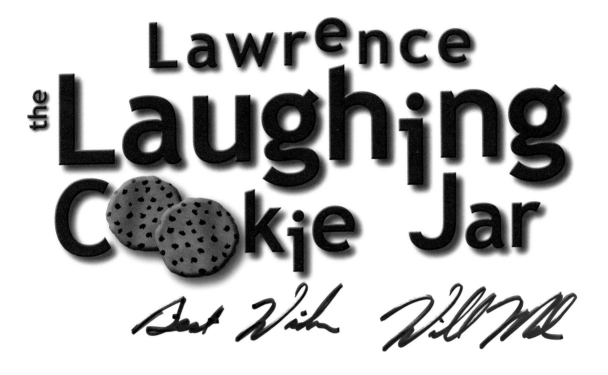

Lawrence the Laughing Cookie Jar

William C. Marks

Illustrations by Josephine Taylor

(MPC) MPC Press International

London   San Francisco   Sydney

Visit us on the Web
www.laughingcookiejar.com

To Mom, Jarkeeper.

Book design and layout by boysaint design
www.boysaint.com

For additional information or copies, contact www.laughingcookiejar.com

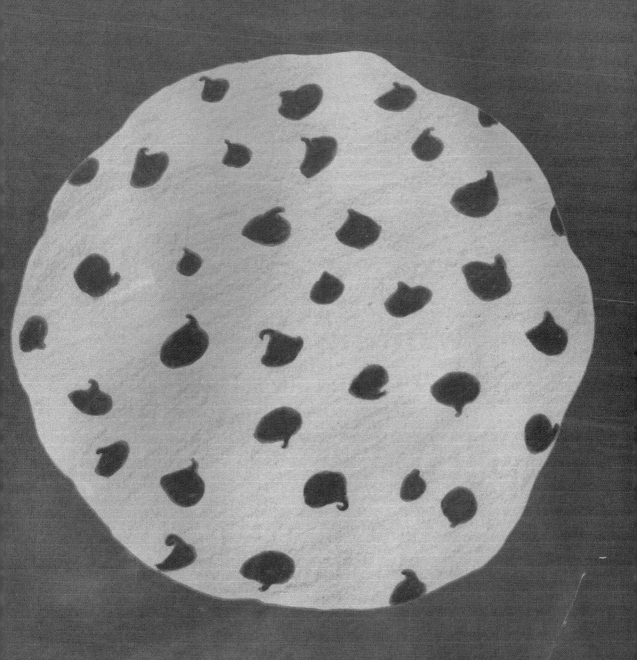

Every cookie lover knows
The story of the Bigelows.

Bud, Ben, and Belle played in the yard.
A child's life was never too hard.
Reggie, the dog, wagging his tail,
Barked "bow-wow" at the man with the mail.

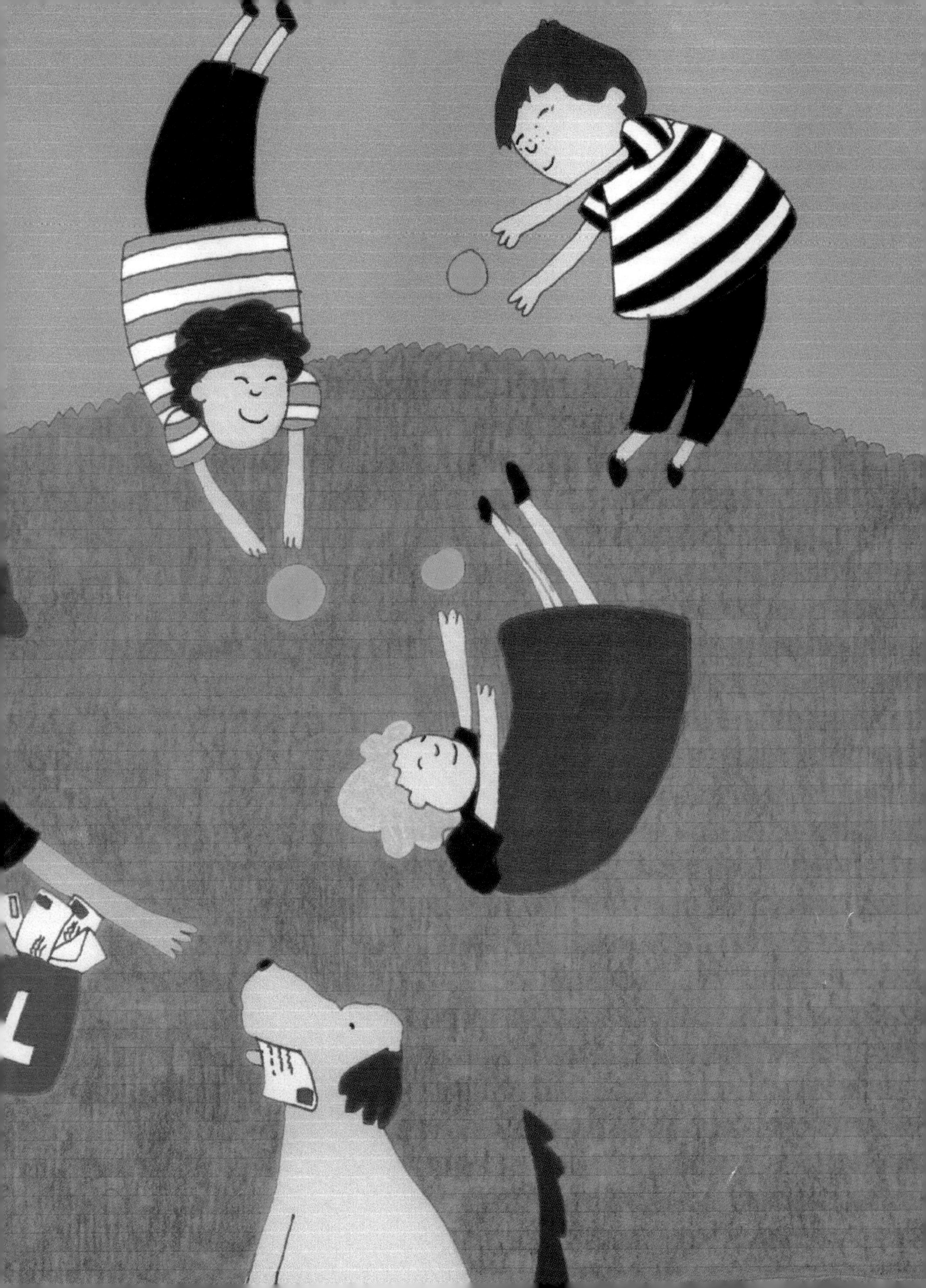

Dinnertime! Each child took a chair
And tasted Mom's delicious fare.

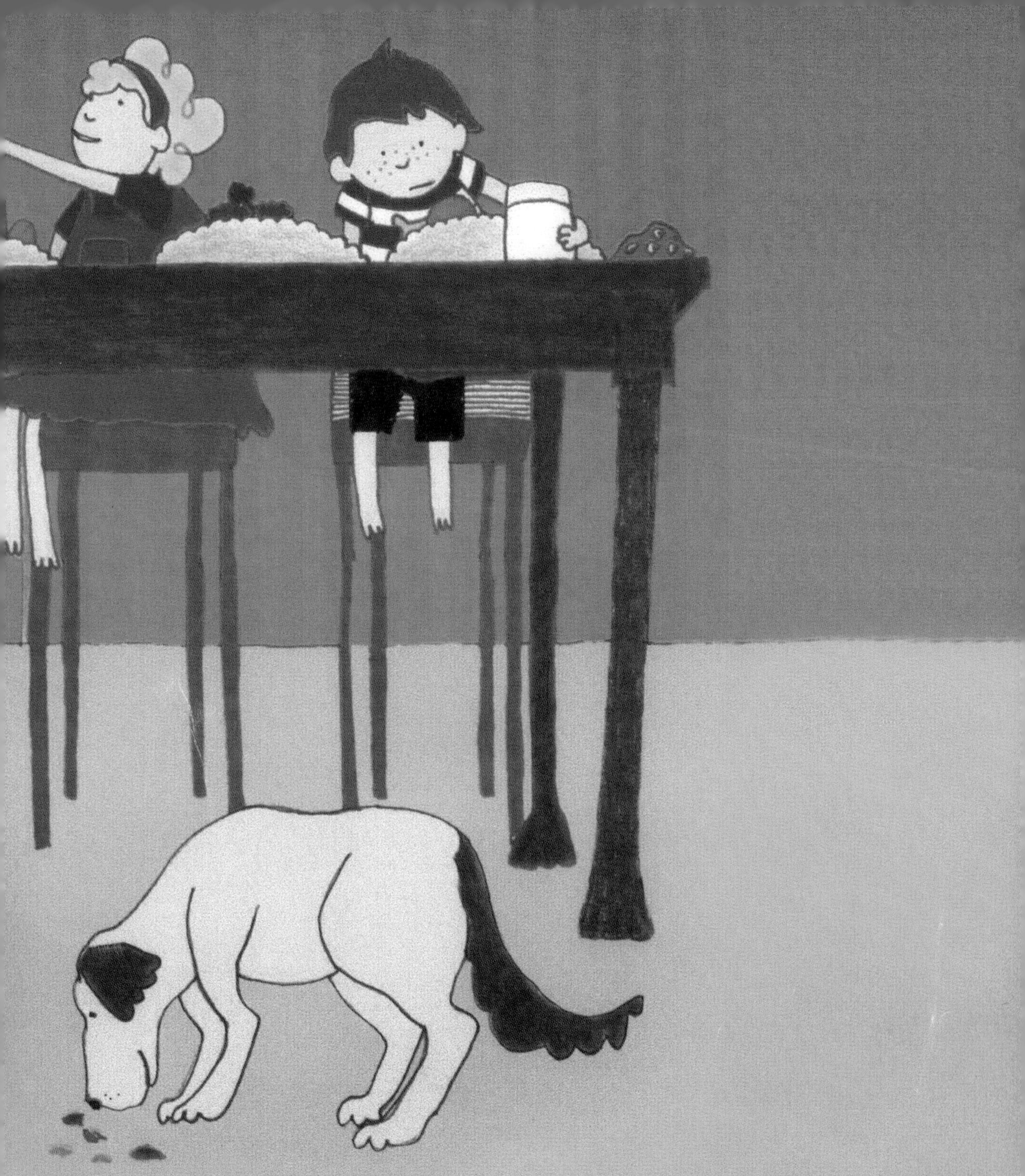

Below the table were three young laps
With hungry Reggie sniffing scraps.

Dessert, of course, was always desired.
"Cookies tonight?" the children inquired.
"Not," said their mom, "'til you clean every plate!"
So they lifted their forks and ate, ate, ate.

But each Bigelow's big tummy
Had room saved for cookies. How yummy!

"Hah Hah! Hee Hee! Har Har!"
It was Lawrence the Laughing Cookie Jar.
When his lid was lifted, a hand reached in
And shifted the cookies to tickle his skin.

Lawrence brought smiles to the saddest of lips
By serving cookies with chocolate chips.

One night, Mom brought out a tray
Of warm-baked cookies made that day.
But she had a rule that was hard to ignore:
The children were offered <u>one</u> cookie, no more.

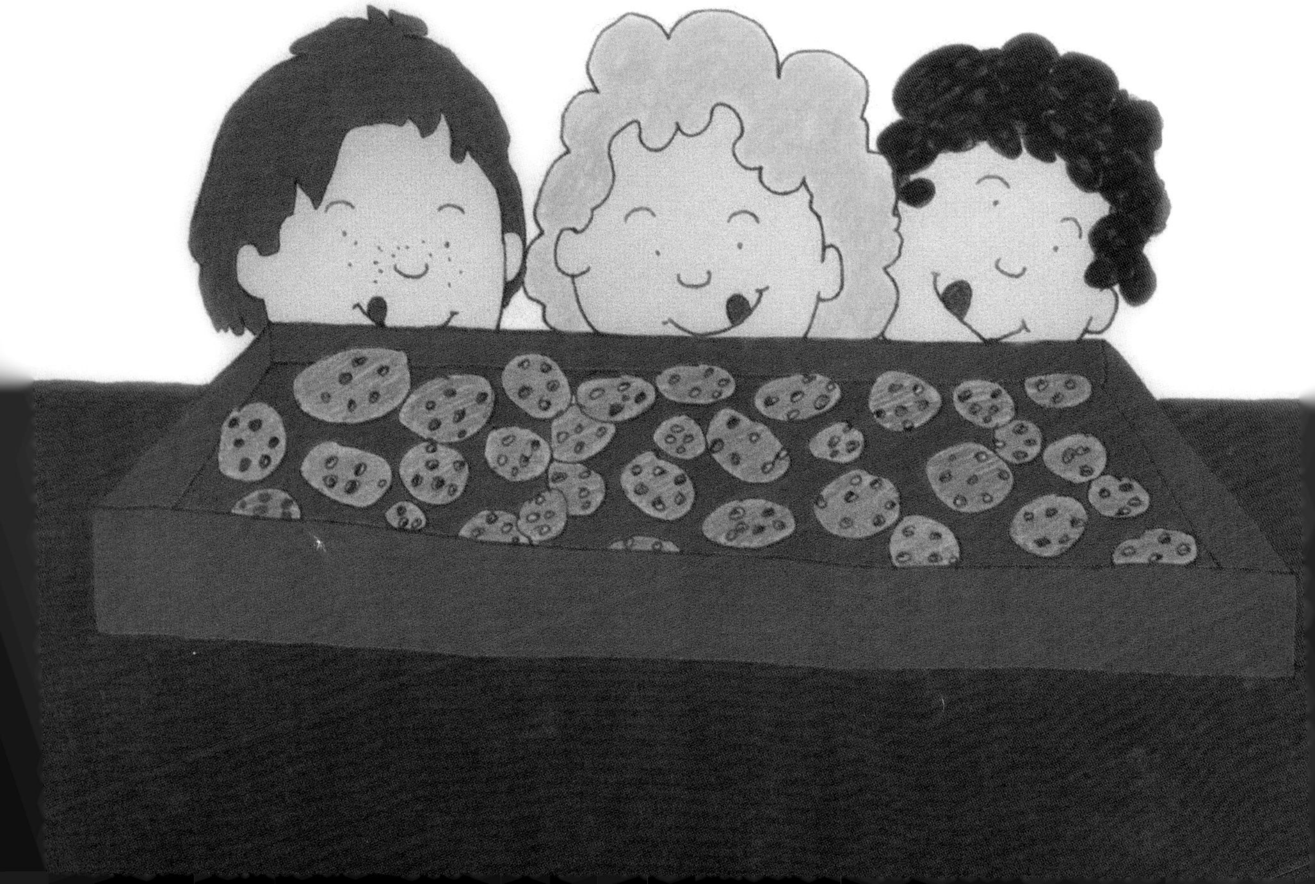

"Mom, just one? Are you sure that is all?
Cookies will help us grow big, strong, and tall."
Mrs. Bigelow stuck to her word.
"Cookies won't help you to grow. How absurd!"

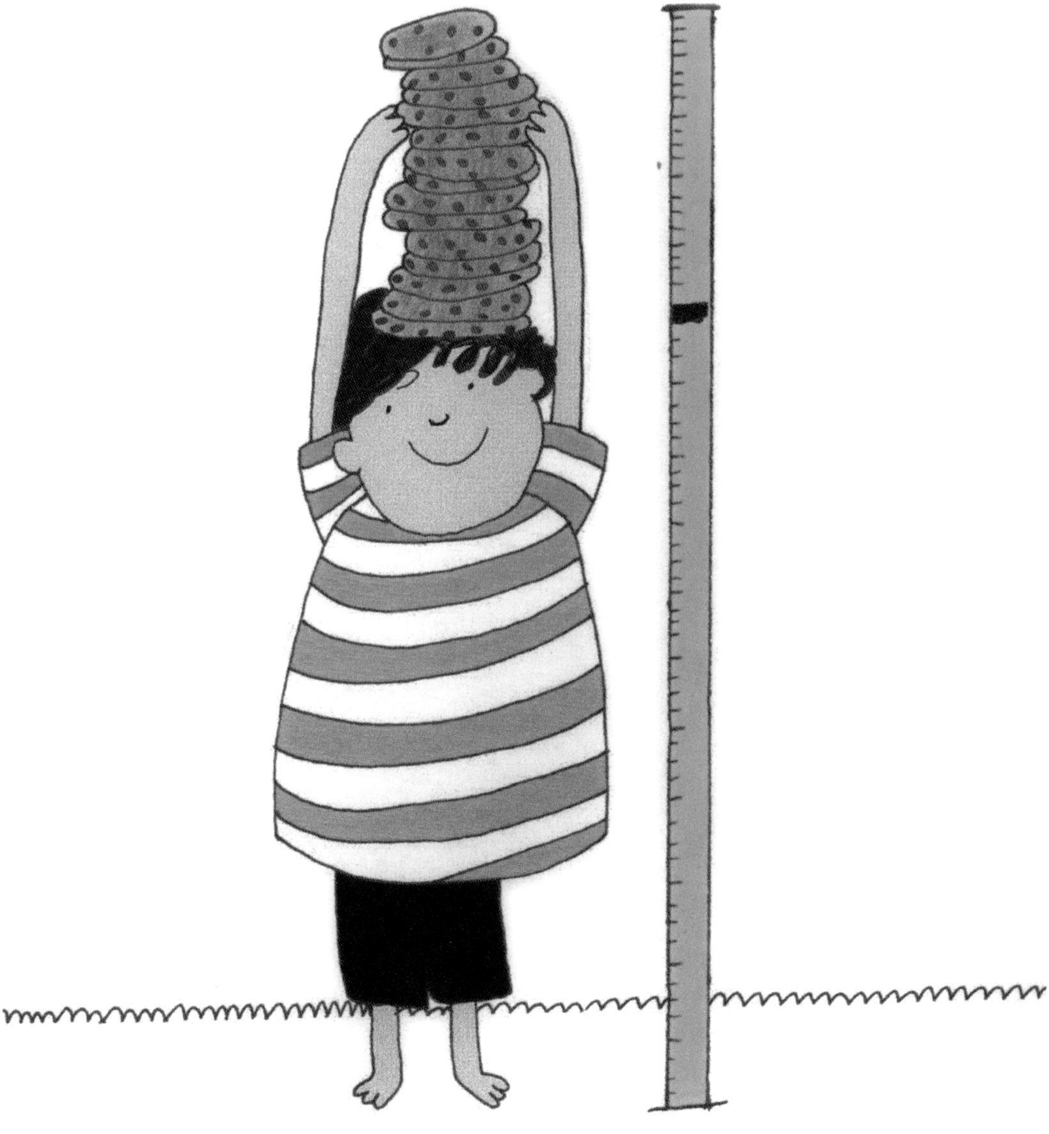

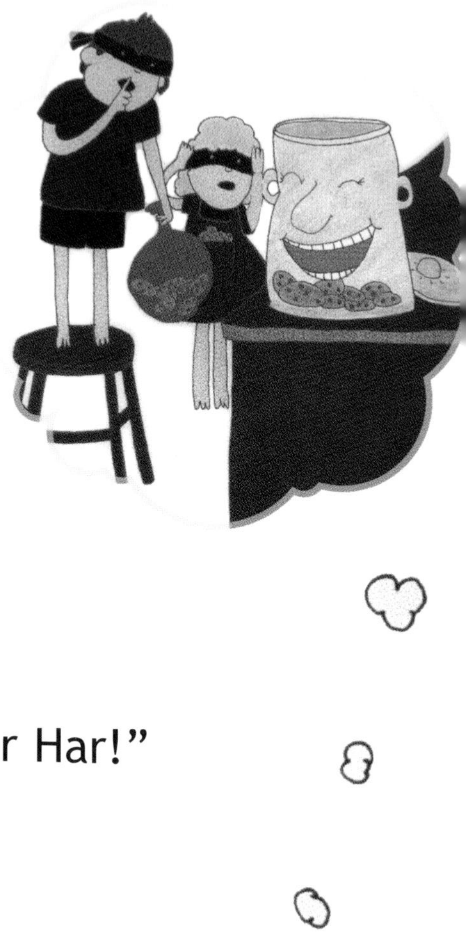

Perhaps it was the perfect time
To try a risky cookie crime.
Yet what about this noisy jar?
So loud, "Hah Hah! Hee Hee! Har Har!"

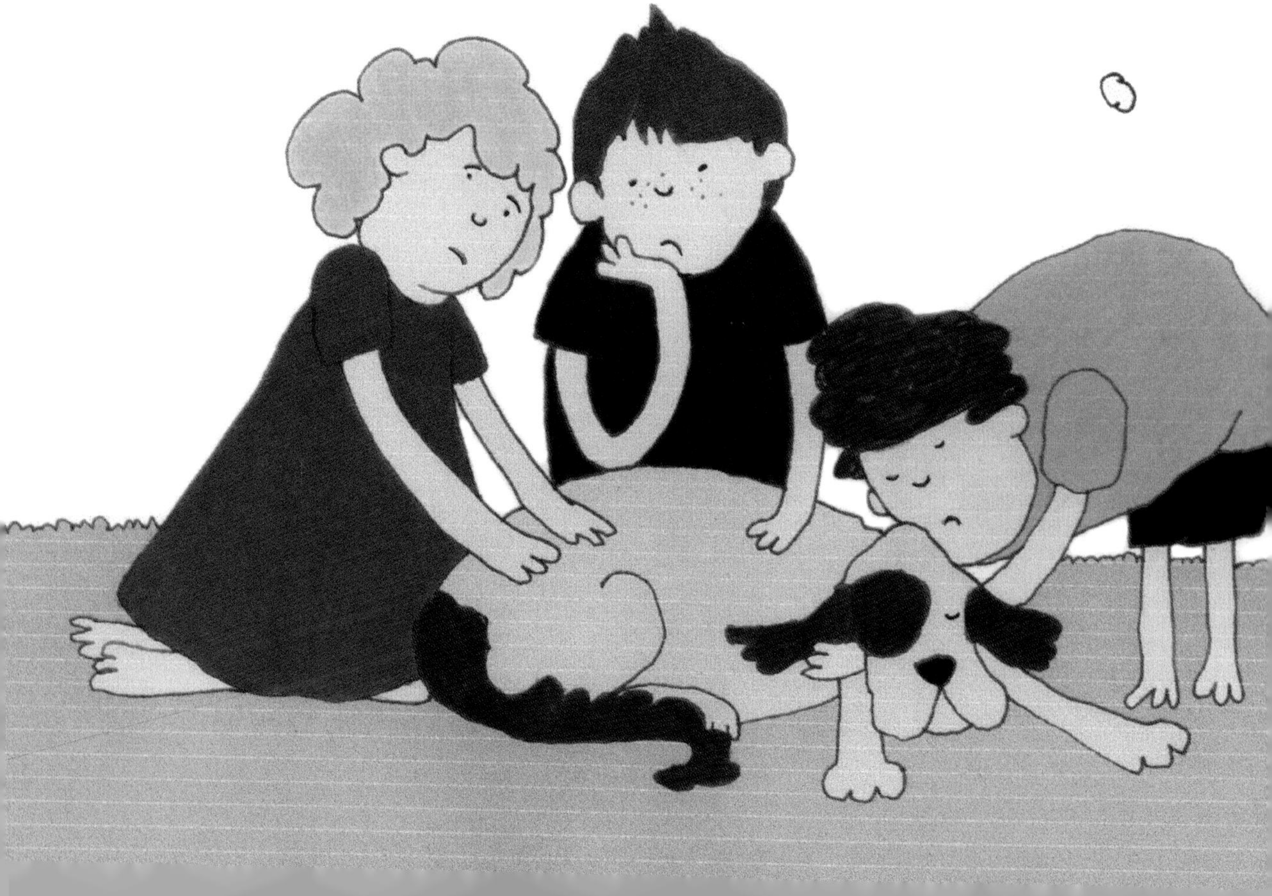

Mom and Dad would hear the laughter.
"Stay out of the jar. We know what you're after!"

But when their parents stepped outside
A secret cookie theft was tried.
The yard was just a little far
To hear "Hah Hah! Hee Hee! Har Har!"

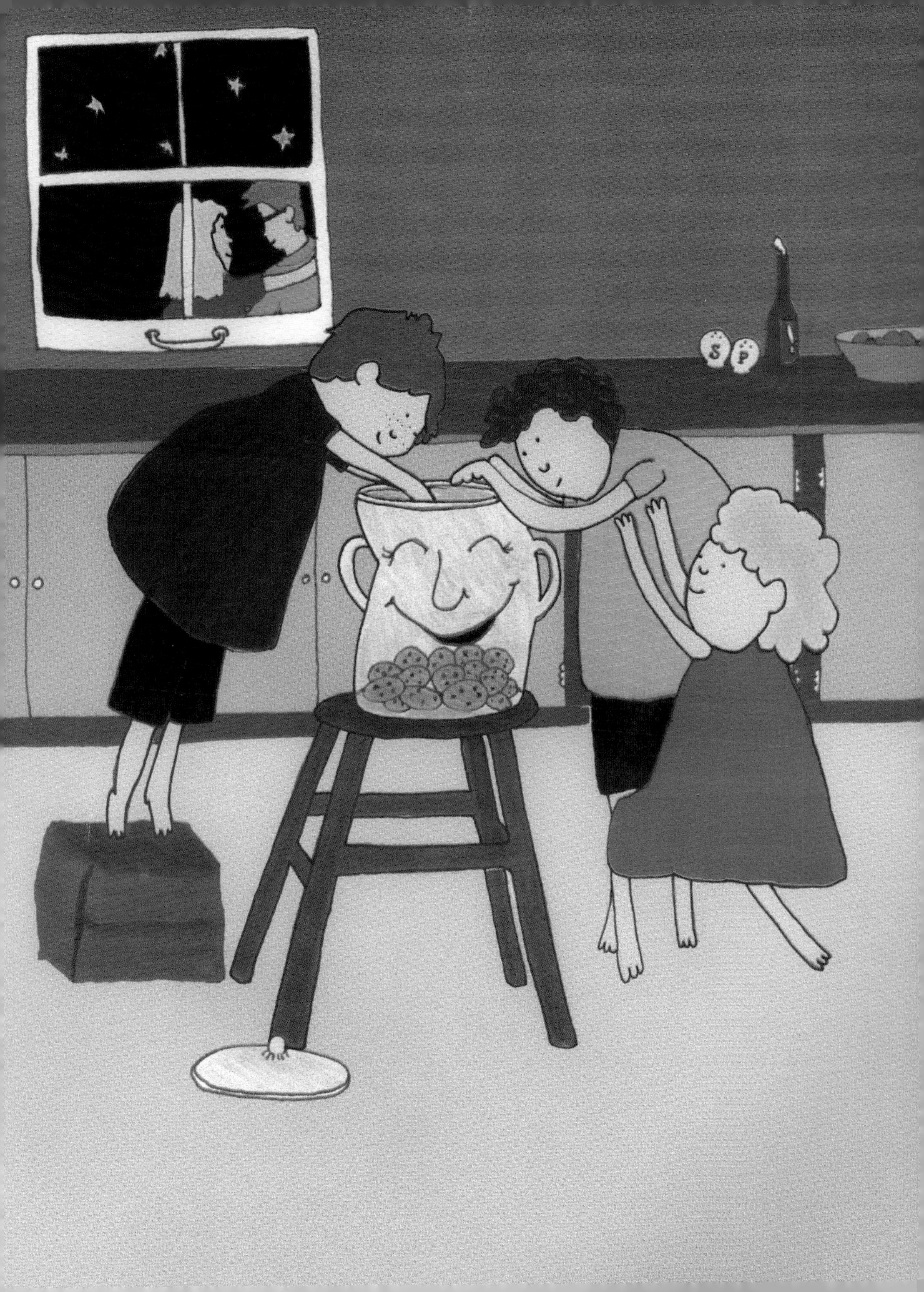
S
P

Now they began to eat, eat, eat
Chocolate chip cookies, semi-sweet!

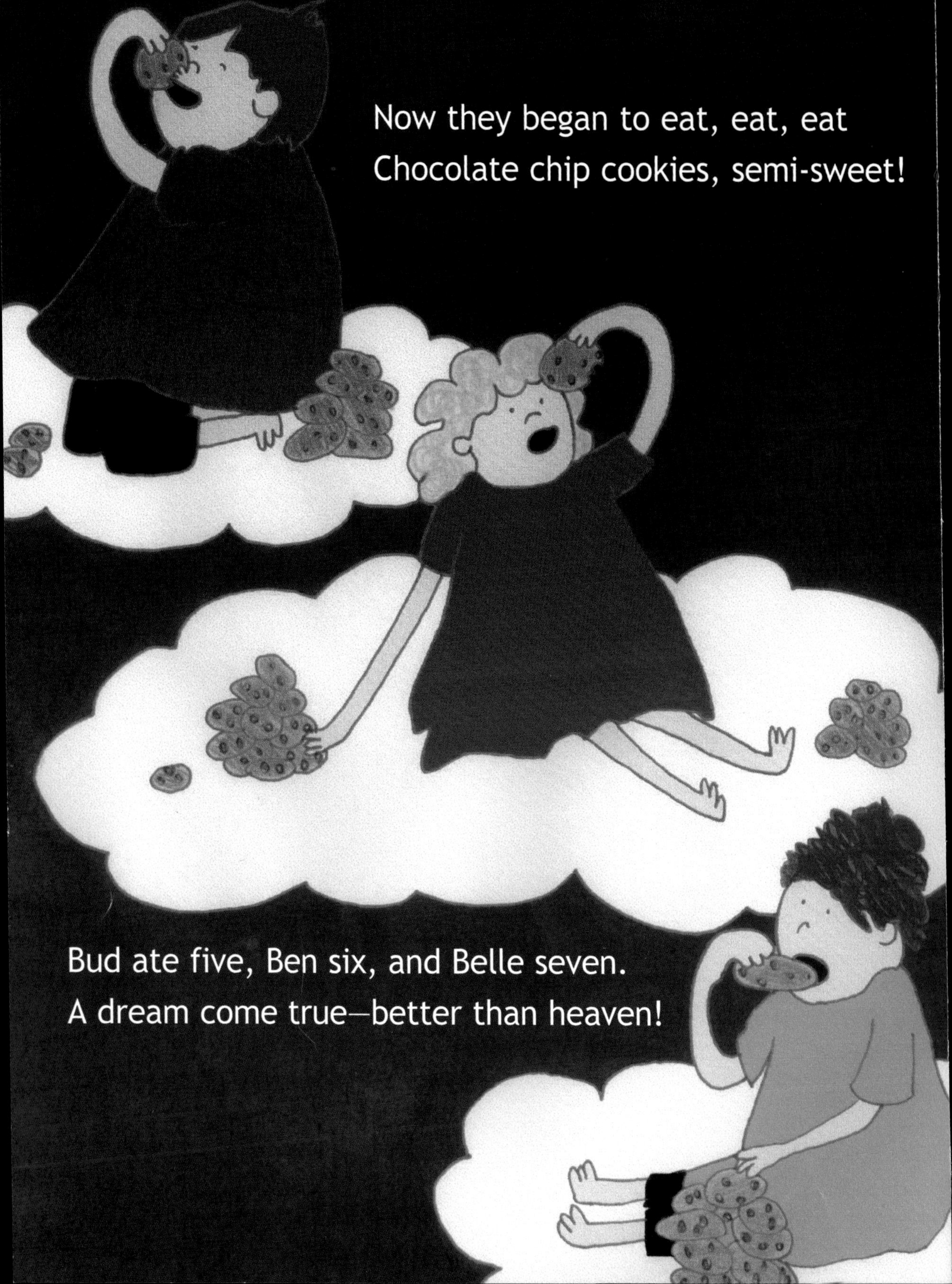

Bud ate five, Ben six, and Belle seven.
A dream come true—better than heaven!

Stomachs were stuffed; they nearly burst.
Glasses of milk helped quench the thirst.

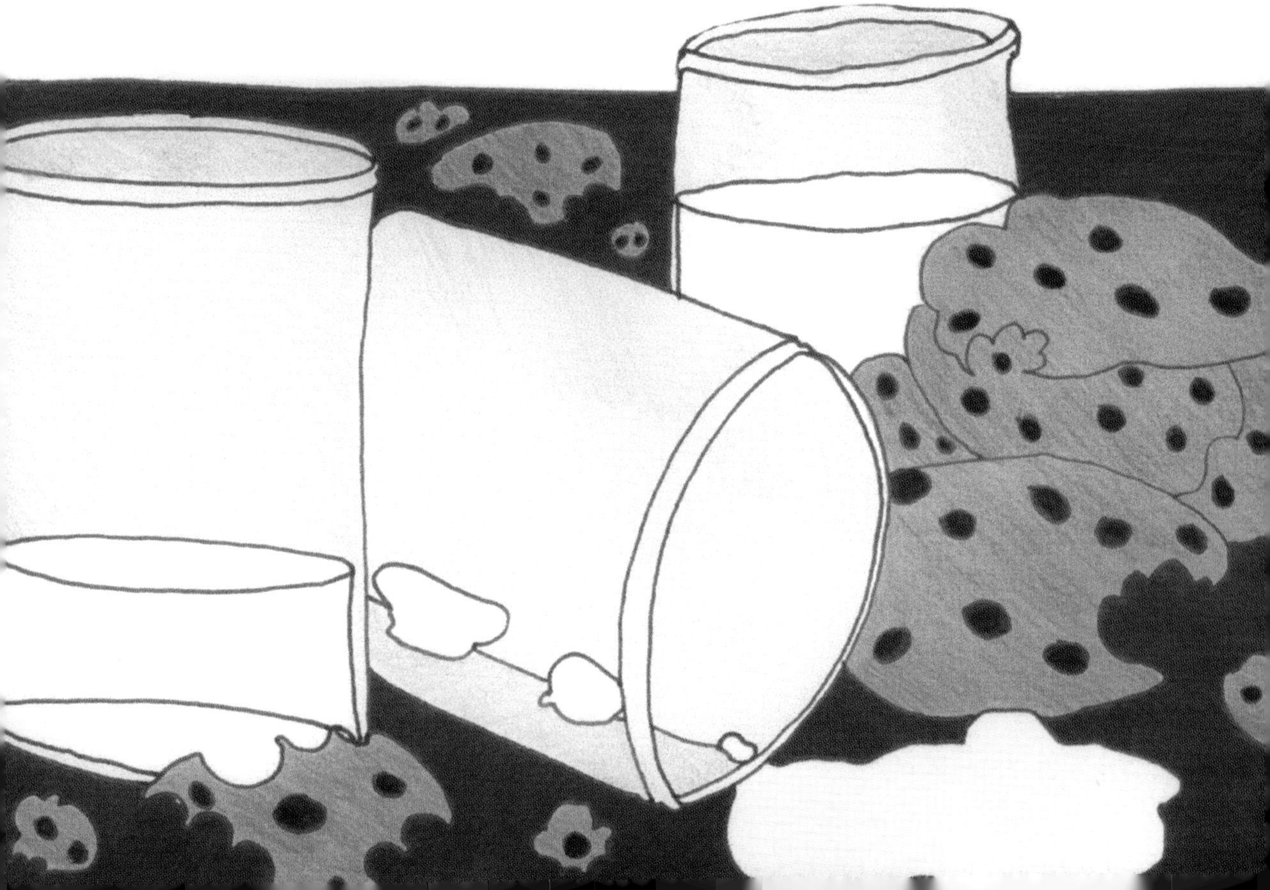

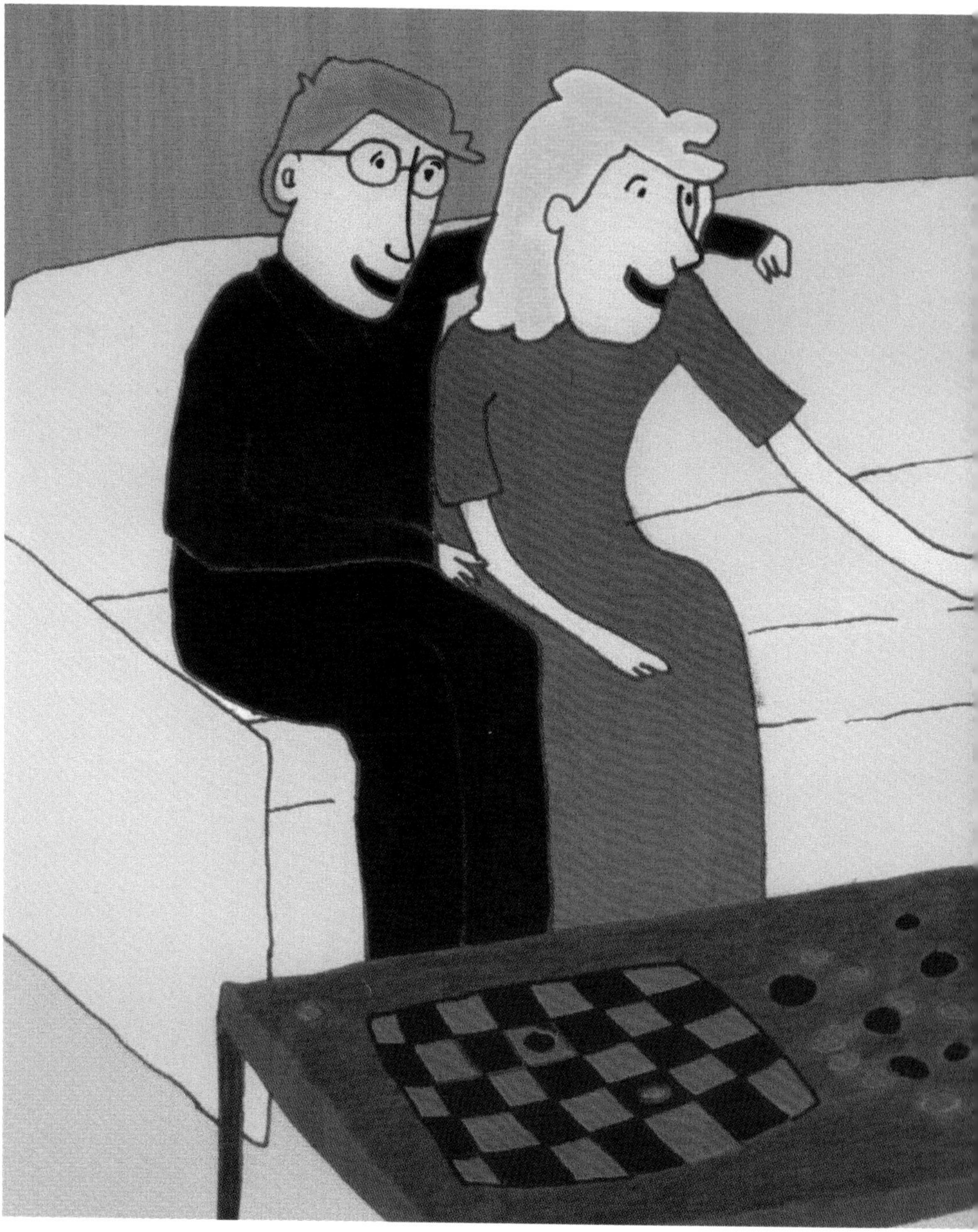

Then through the house they heard their names.
"Bud! Ben! Belle! Come play some games!"

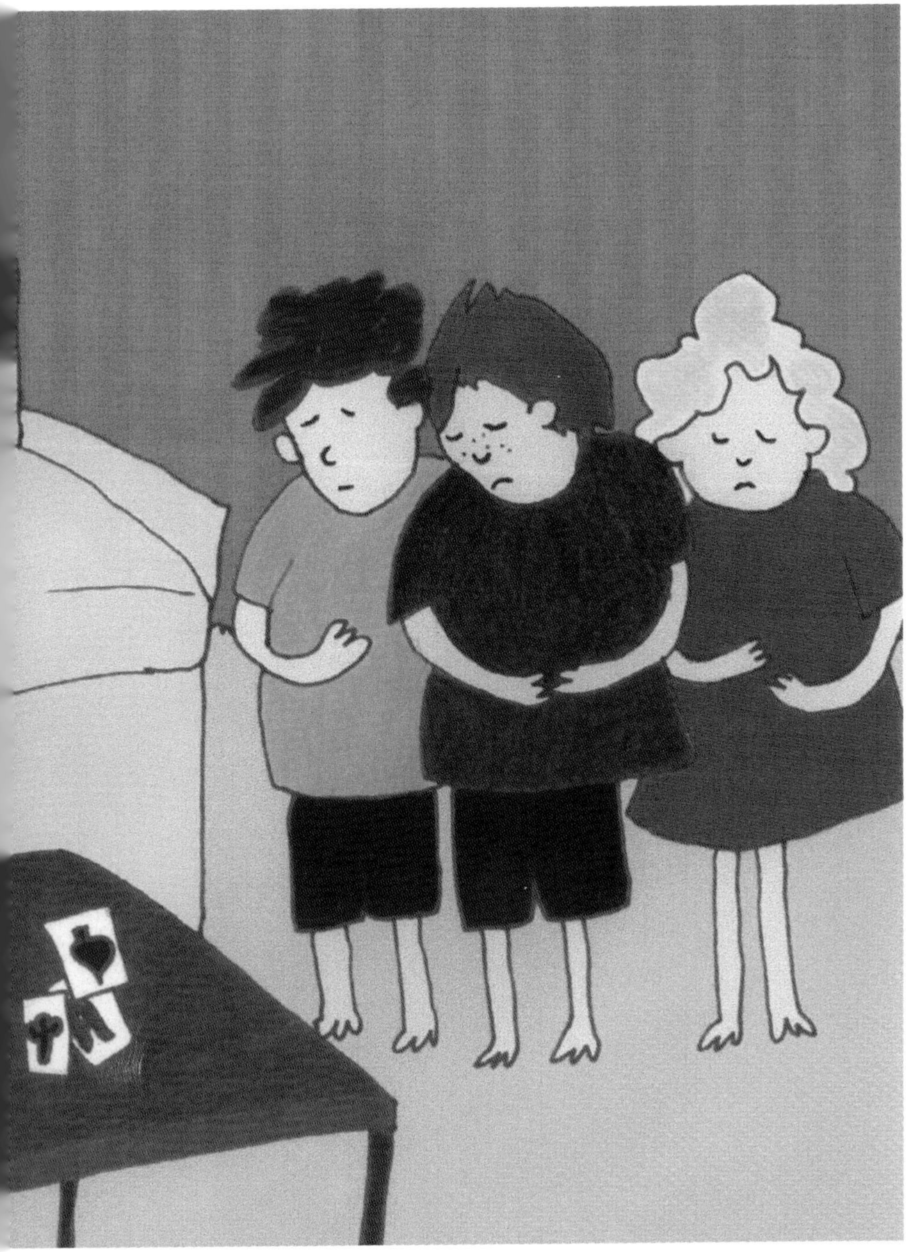

Three voices whimpered, "Mom, Dad,
Our stomachs feel so awfully bad."
With that, they were off to their beds,
Three sick stomachs, three sleepy heads.

Lying awake
With three times an ache,
They tossed and turned.
Their bellies bubbled and burned
And were ready to pop!
The pain did not stop.

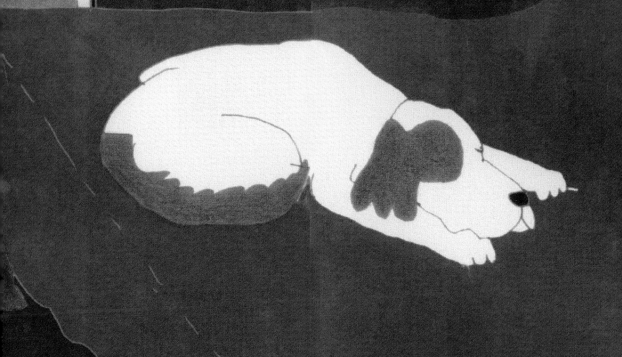

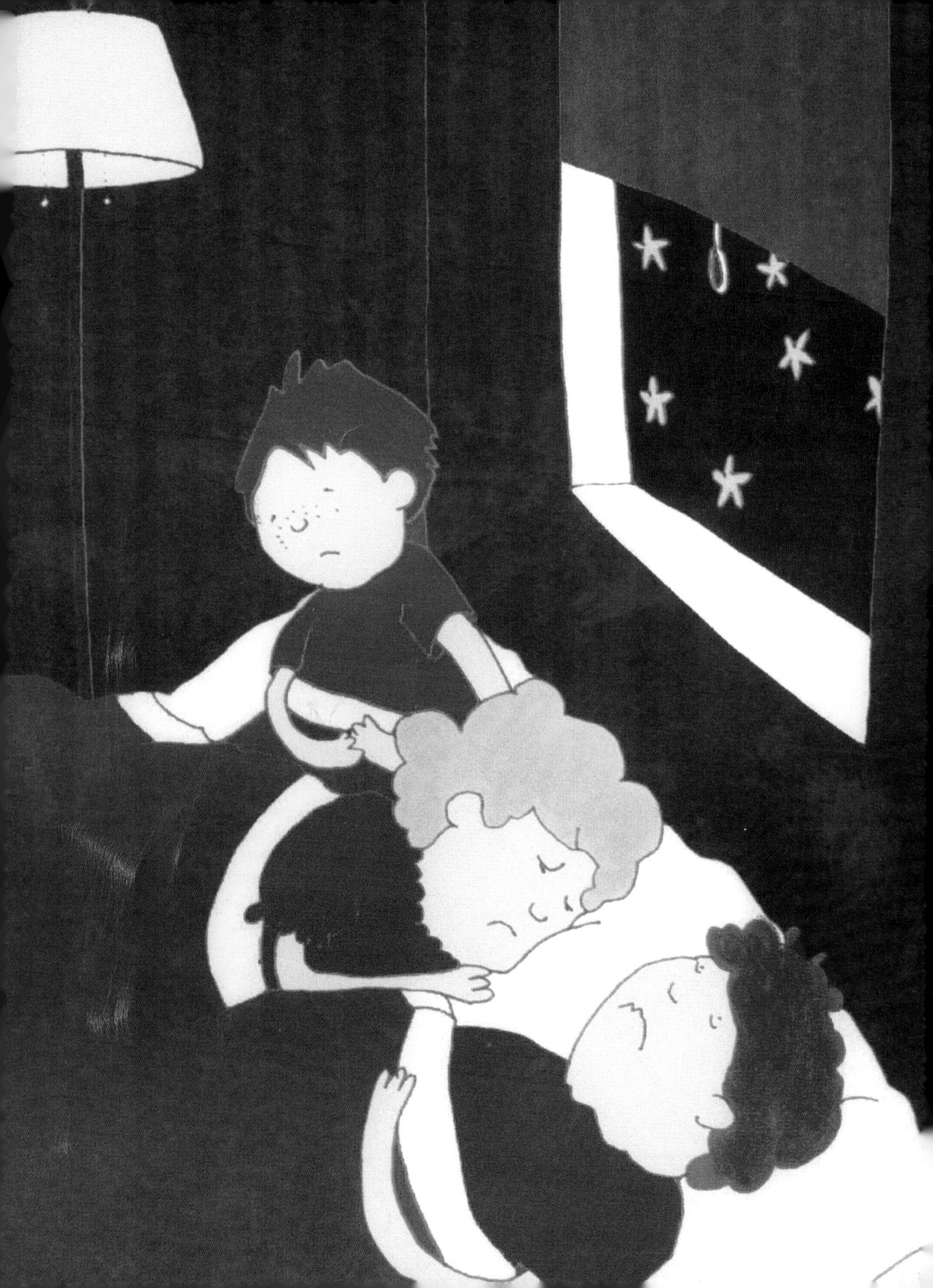

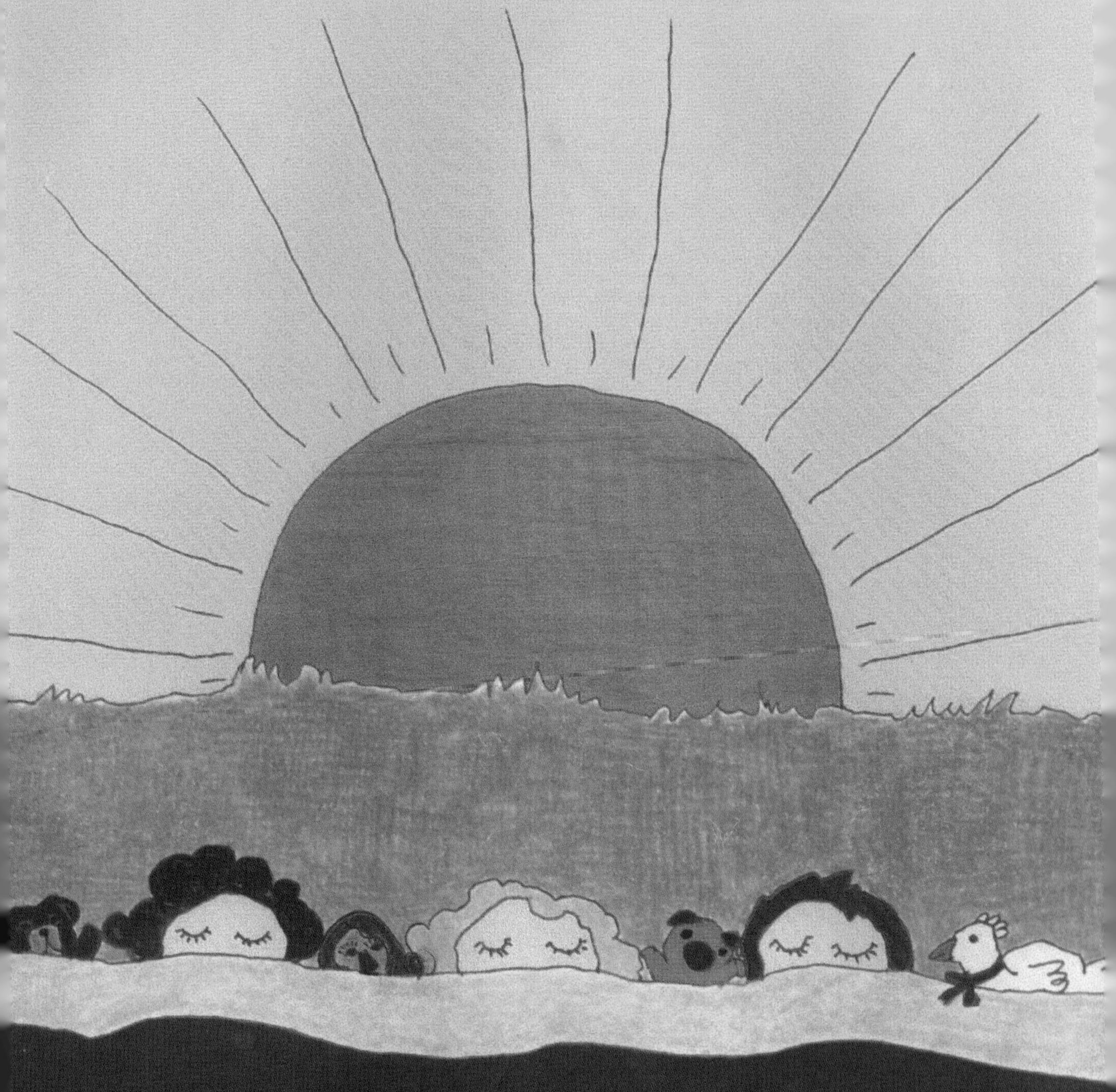

The sun rose, and the children did not.
They lay in their beds, a sad, sickly lot.

Hours later, they awoke
To groans and growls. Their stomachs spoke!
"Oooh! Argh! Uggh! Owww!
Why can't this awful hurt stop now?"

Under the sheets, they stayed through lunch.
Sandwiches, chips, strawberry punch,
And cake topped with chocolate fudge!
But not one Bigelow would budge.

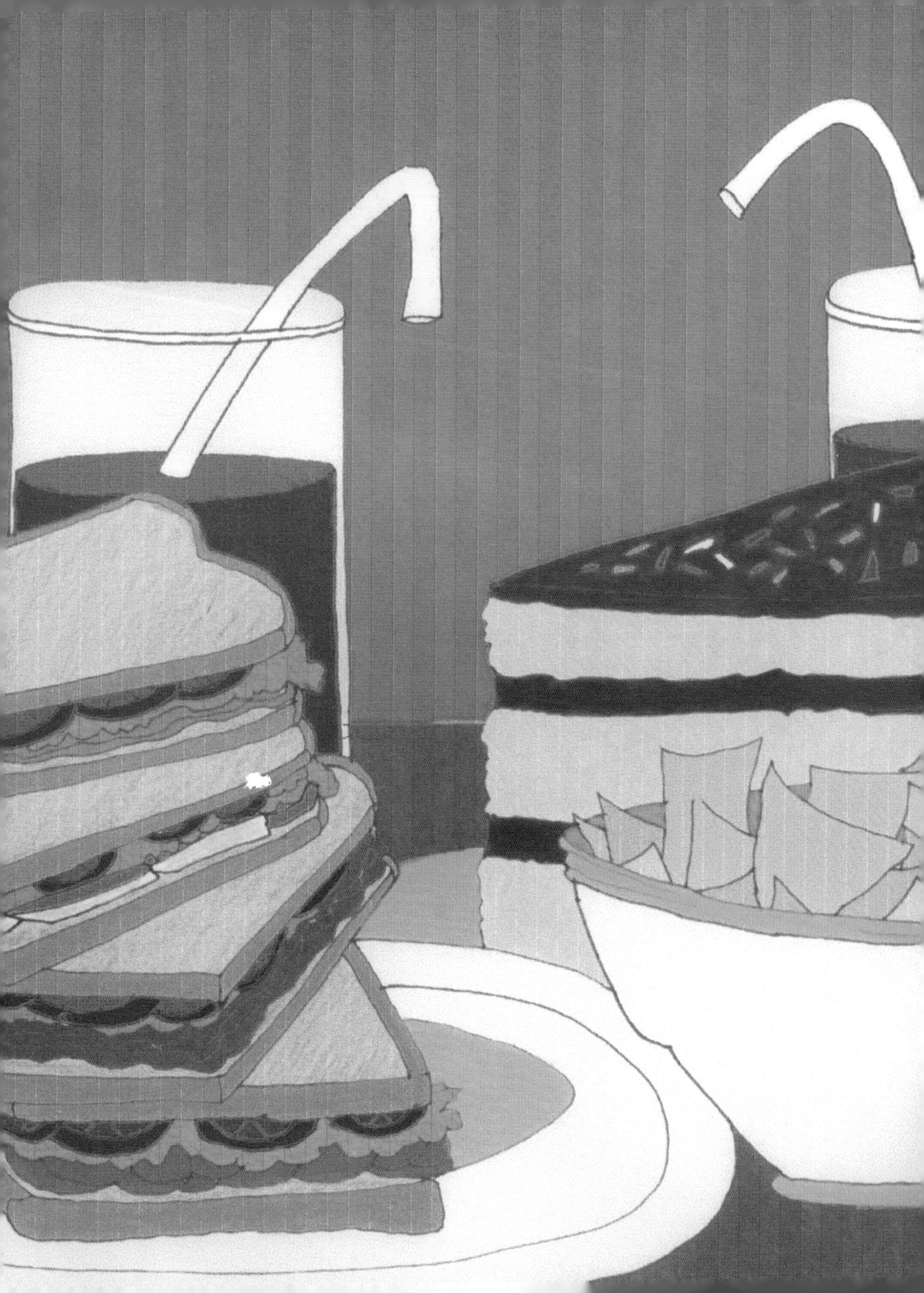

By dinnertime, the children found
Their appetites had come around.
Mother knew that they were ready
For their favorite dish, spaghetti.

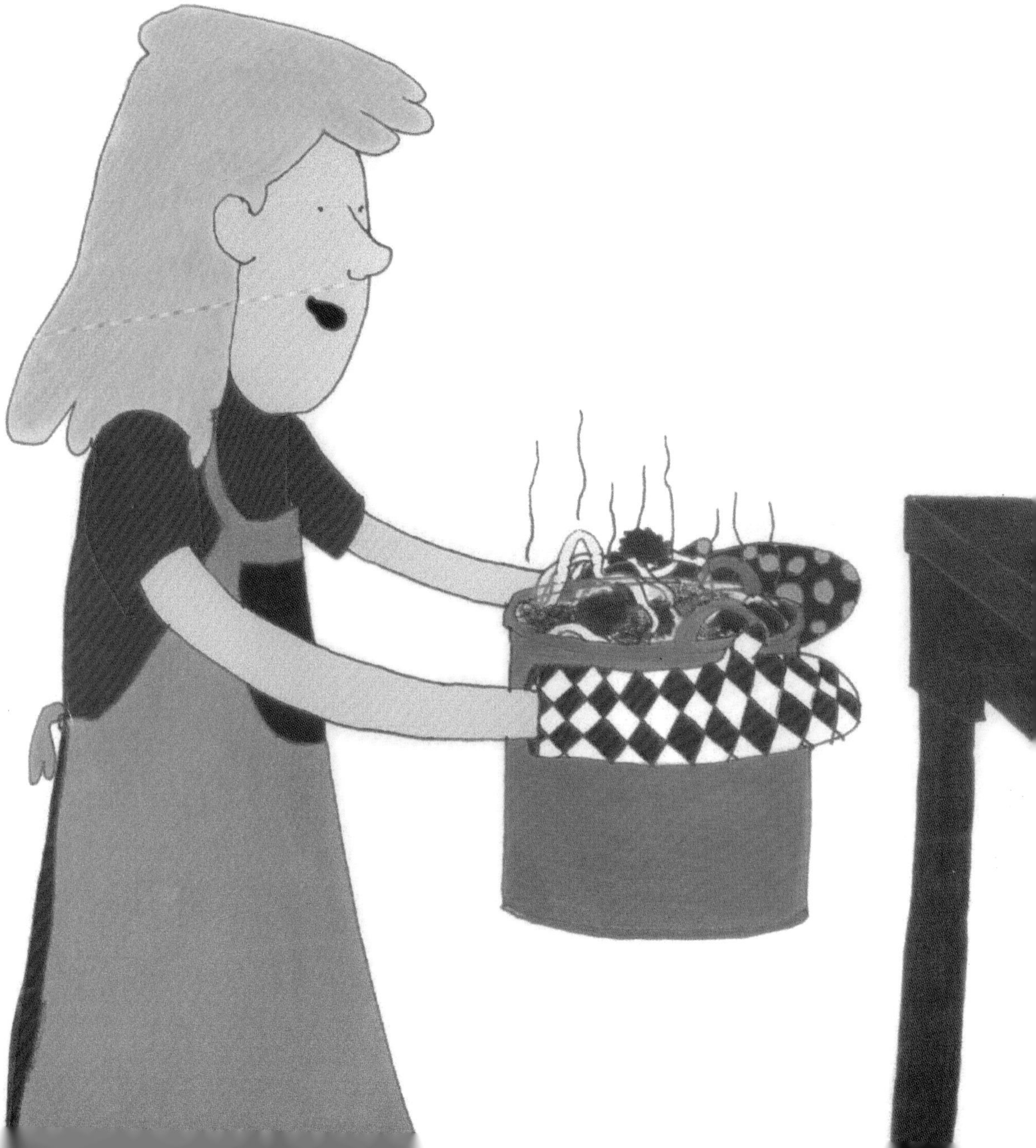

As well, there were some healthy greens.
The vegetables that night were beans.

And three happy stomachs that no longer hurt
Were offered warm cookies Mom baked for dessert.

"Dessert? Oh Mother, that is nice.
A single cookie will suffice!"
So very quickly Mom could tell,
Her children learned a lesson well.

But when she went to pick out three
Of her fine treats, what did Mom see?
Just two small cookies were still left.
Was it another cookie theft?

Yes it was, and it happened when
She wandered in the yard again.
Too far to hear the laughing jar,
A loud "Hah Hah! Hee Hee! Har Har!"

"Three thieves once more? I must be wrong.
They were bed-bound all day long."

The father said, "It was not I."
And he had never told a lie.

Said Ben, "I know who gives us grief.
That cold-nosed, hairy cookie thief!

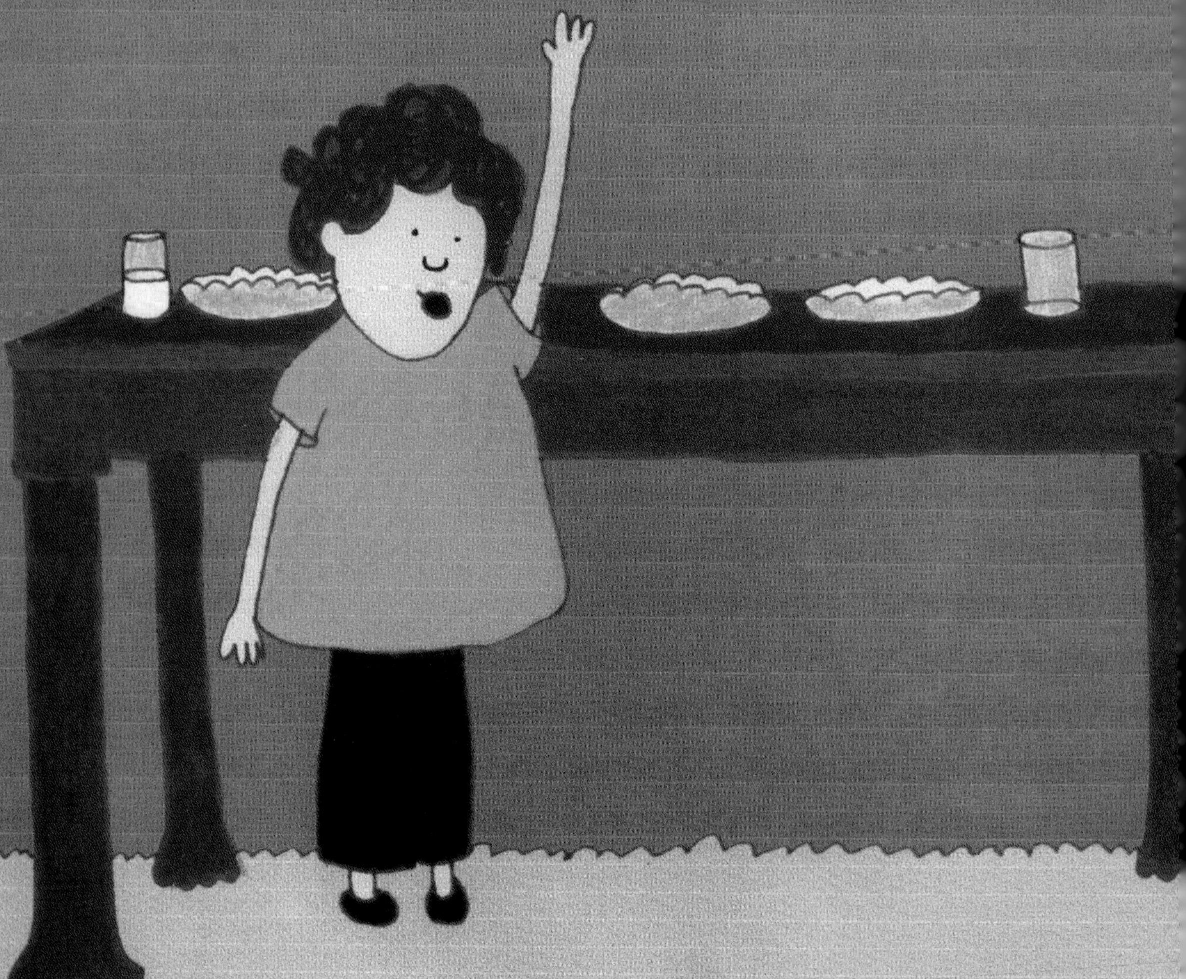

Throughout the meal he always begs
And sniffs the floor beneath my legs.
When Reggie's not here looking for food,
He must be up to no good, I conclude."

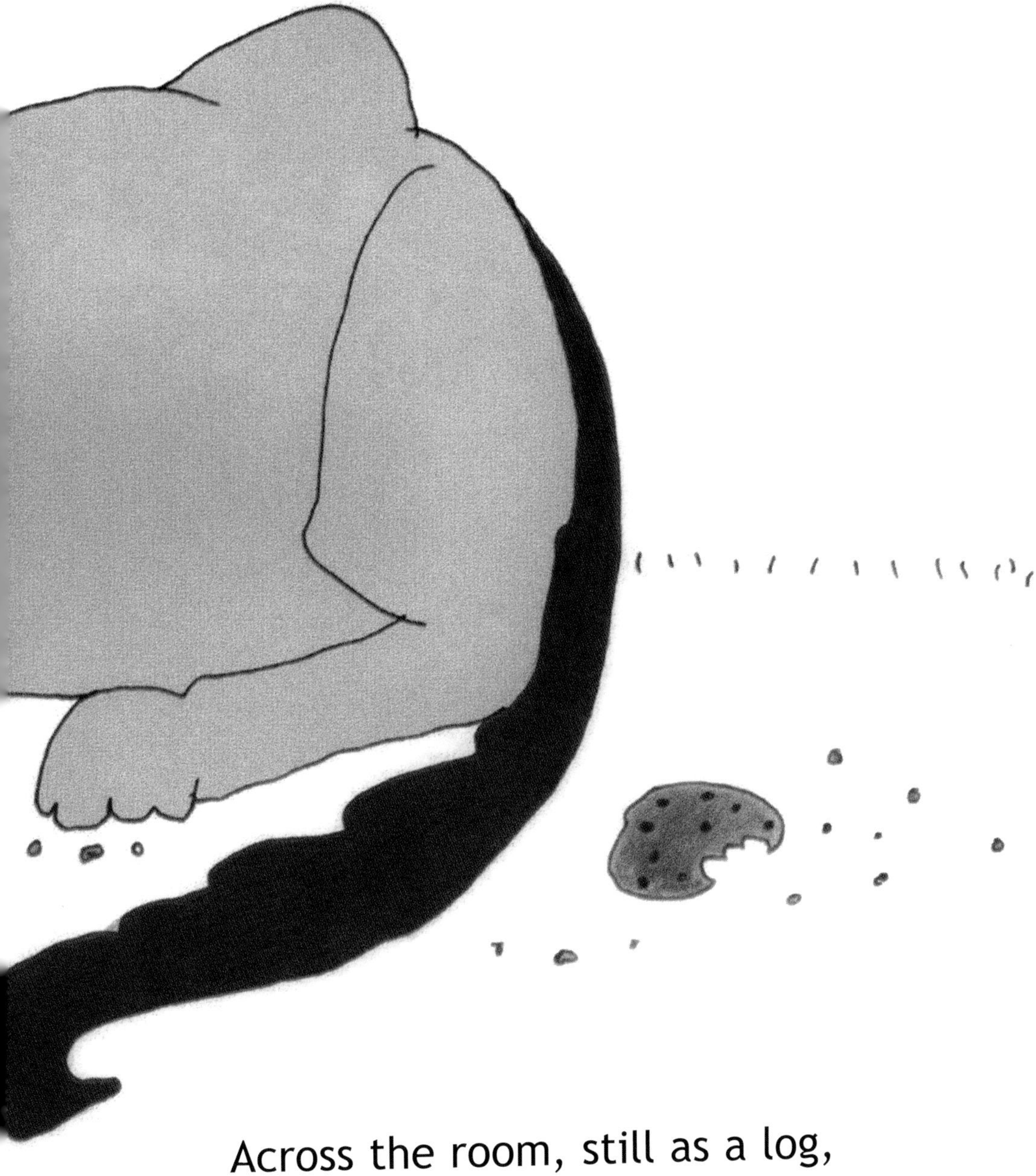

Across the room, still as a log,
Poor Reggie lay, sick as a dog.
Guilty? Oh yes! Look what they saw—
Cookie crumbs were stuck to his paw.

Two days passed as Reggie rested.
Uggh! His stomach had been tested.
No doggy chow. No doggy bone.
He learned a lesson of his own.

Today the dog is feeling good.
He runs around the neighborhood.
As for the three young cookie thieves,
The love of cookies never leaves.
Listen. You can hear the jar,
"Hah Hah! Hee Hee! Har Har!"

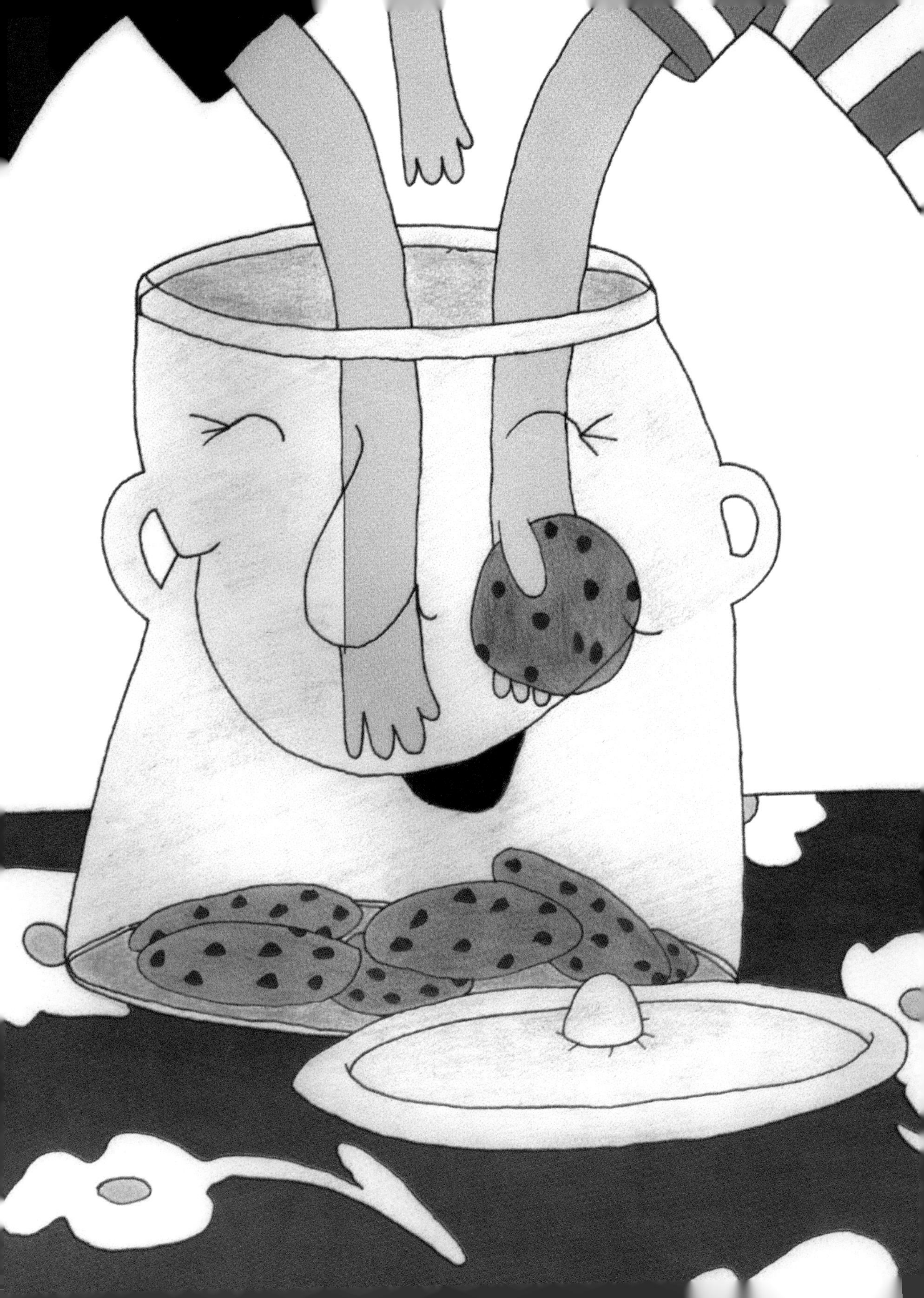